TORTOISE'S DREAM

Joanna Troughton

Author's Note
The story of the miraculous tree, and of Tortoise who remembered its name, comes from the Bantu people of Africa. Many different versions are told in places as far apart as Cameroun in the north and Transvaal in the south.

Tortoise had a dream.

He dreamt of a tree which
was in a secret place.
From the tree's branches grew
all the fruits of the earth —
bananas, dates, coconuts, melons,
millet, yams, cassava, maize,
pineapples and oranges.

Tortoise told the animals about the tree of his
dream. "From its branches grow—bananas, dates,
coconuts, melons, millet, yams, cassava, maize,
pineapples and oranges."
The Lion laughed. "It's only a dream," he said.
"No," said Tortoise. "It is real. I will go to
Grandmother Koko. She will know where it grows."
"You are too slow and steady," said the Lion.
"I will go myself."

The Lion went.

He told Grandmother Koko about Tortoise's dream.
"I have heard of this tree," said Grandmother Koko.
"Its name is Omumbo-rombonga. But if you want the
fruit to fall you must call out its name."
"Omumbo-rombonga," said the Lion. "How shall I
find the tree?"
"If you remember the name you will find the tree.
If you remember the name the fruit will fall,"
said Grandmother Koko. "But don't look round on
your way back or the name will go out of your head."

The Lion was fierce and he was bold.
He wouldn't forget the name.
"Omumbo-rombonga," he said.
But on his way back he looked round . . .

THUD! He tripped over an ant hill.
The name went out of his head.
"Omrongbing . . .?"

Next went the Elephant.
"Mind the ant hill," said the Lion.
"The name of the tree is Omumbo-rombonga,"
said Grandmother Koko. "And don't look round."

The Elephant was big and he was strong. He wouldn't forget the name. "Omumbo-rombonga," he said. On his way back he saw the ant hill. But then he looked round . . . OUCH! He trod on a thorn instead. The name went out of his head. "Bongarombo . . .?"

Next went the Hyena.
"Mind the thorn," said
the Elephant.
"The name of the tree is
Omumbo-rombonga," said
Grandmother Koko. "And don't
look round."
The Hyena was cunning and she
was sly. She wouldn't forget
the name.
"Omumbo-rombonga," she said.
She saw the ant hill.
She saw the thorn.
But then she looked round . . .

SPLASH! She fell into
a pool of water.
The name went out
of her head.
"Bing-bong-bang . . .?"

Next went the Ostrich.

"Mind the pool," said the Hyena.

"The name of the tree is Omumbo-rombonga,"
said Grandmother Koko. "And don't look round."
The Ostrich was fast and he was speedy. He
wouldn't forget the name.

"Omumbo-rombonga," he said.

He saw the ant hill.

He saw the thorn.

He saw the pool.

But then he looked round—HISSS! There was a
large snake at his feet. The name went out of
his head.

"Mabomba . . .?"

Next went the Baboon.
"Mind the snake,"
said the Ostrich.

"The name of the tree
is Omumbo-rombonga,"
said Grandmother Koko.
"And don't look round . . ."

The Baboon was clever
and he was wise. He
wouldn't forget the name.
"Omumbo-rombonga," he sa

He saw the ant hill.

He saw the thorn.

He saw the pool.

He saw the snake.

But then he looked round . . .

SWISH! He was caught
in a creeper.

The name went out of his head.
"Mumbo-bumbo . . .?"

Next went the Giraffe.
"Mind the creeper,"
said the Baboon.
"The name of the tree
is Omumbo-rombonga,"
said Grandmother Koko.
"And don't look round."
The Giraffe was stately
and she was proud. She
wouldn't forget the name.
"Omumbo-rombonga,"
she said.
She saw the ant hill.
She saw the thorn.
She saw the pool.
She saw the snake.
She saw the creeper.
But then she looked
round . . .
SPLAT! She slipped on
a patch of mud.
The name went out of
her head.
"Mim-bim-obo . . .?"

"Please let me go," said Tortoise.
The animals let him go.
"Mind the mud," said the Giraffe.
"The name of the tree is
Omumbo-rombonga," said Grandmother
Koko. "And don't look round."
Tortoise was slow and he was
steady. He wouldn't forget the
name. "Omumbo-rombonga," he said.

He saw the ant hill.
He saw the thorn.
He saw the pool.

He saw the snake.
He saw the creeper.

He saw the mud . . .

And he didn't look round.

So he saw the scorpion in his path.
"Lucky I didn't look round," thought Tortoise.
"Omumbo-rombonga," he said to himself.

"Have you remembered the name?"
said the animals, as they saw
Tortoise slowly and steadily coming.
"Look behind you," said Tortoise.

And there was the Omumbo-rombonga tree. From its branches grew bananas, dates, coconuts, melons, millet, yams, cassava, maize, pineapples and oranges.

"Omumbo-rombonga," cried Tortoise.

Down showered the bananas,
the dates, the coconuts, the melons,
the millet, the yams, the cassava,
the maize, the pineapples and the oranges.

After the animals had eaten,
Tortoise said, "Let everyone
plant a seed."

The seeds grew. So now the
animals have food of their
own, grown from the fruits of
the Omumbo-rombonga tree.